This Little Tiger book belongs to:

_____

_____

_____

For Kath, Justine and Andrea
~ C F

For Dusty
~ R T

LITTLE TIGER PRESS
1 The Coda Centre, 189 Munster Road,
London SW6 6AW
www.littletigerpress.com

First published in Great Britain 2004
This edition published 2012
by Little Tiger Press, London

ISBN 978-1-84506-009-1
Printed in China
LTP/1900/0460/0512
10 9 8 7 6 5 4 3 2 1

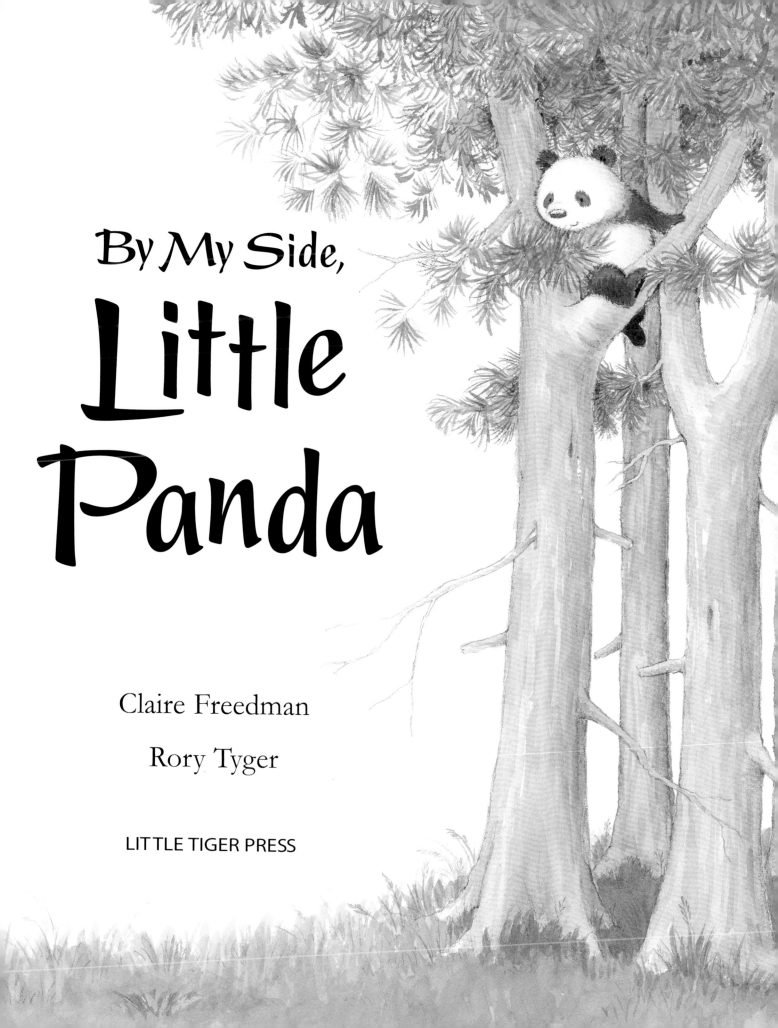

By My Side, Little Panda

Claire Freedman

Rory Tyger

LITTLE TIGER PRESS

Little Panda and his mother did everything together.
Together they explored the mountain tops,
where the snow lay too deep to melt.

Together, they splashed in icy streams,
startling tiny, shiny fish . . .

and rolled down grassy slopes,
carpeted with early spring flowers.

And as the first stars peeped out above
the snowy crags, they were still together,
snuggled up tight.

"The world is full of wonders for
a brave little panda bear like you,"
said Mother Panda. "You'll discover echoing
caves where butterflies hide. You'll play in
sparkling waterfalls, and climb trees so high
you can almost touch the clouds!"

"Will I really do all that?" cried
Little Panda.

"One day!" Mother Panda laughed.

And soon Little Panda was asleep,
dreaming of dancing butterflies!

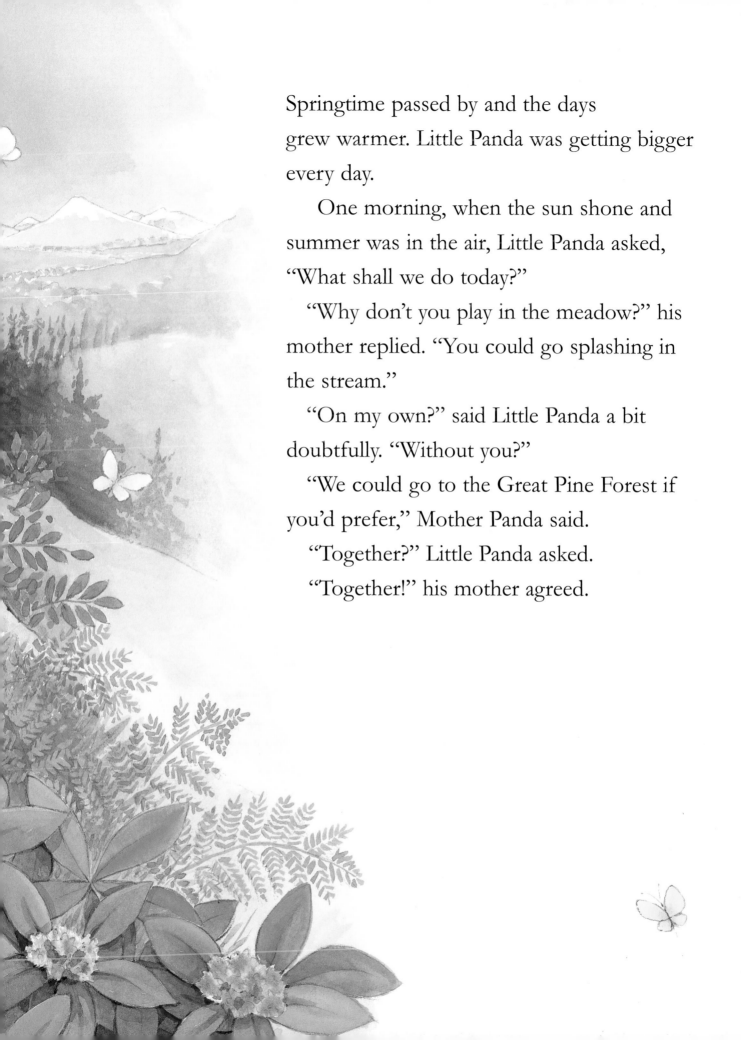

Springtime passed by and the days grew warmer. Little Panda was getting bigger every day.

One morning, when the sun shone and summer was in the air, Little Panda asked, "What shall we do today?"

"Why don't you play in the meadow?" his mother replied. "You could go splashing in the stream."

"On my own?" said Little Panda a bit doubtfully. "Without you?"

"We could go to the Great Pine Forest if you'd prefer," Mother Panda said.

"Together?" Little Panda asked.

"Together!" his mother agreed.

Little Panda had never been in the
Great Pine Forest before.

Golden monkeys with bright blue faces
leaped through the leafy trees. Soft brown
musk deer peeped out from the misty shadows
and beautiful birds fluttered across their path.

Little Panda's eyes shone with excitement.

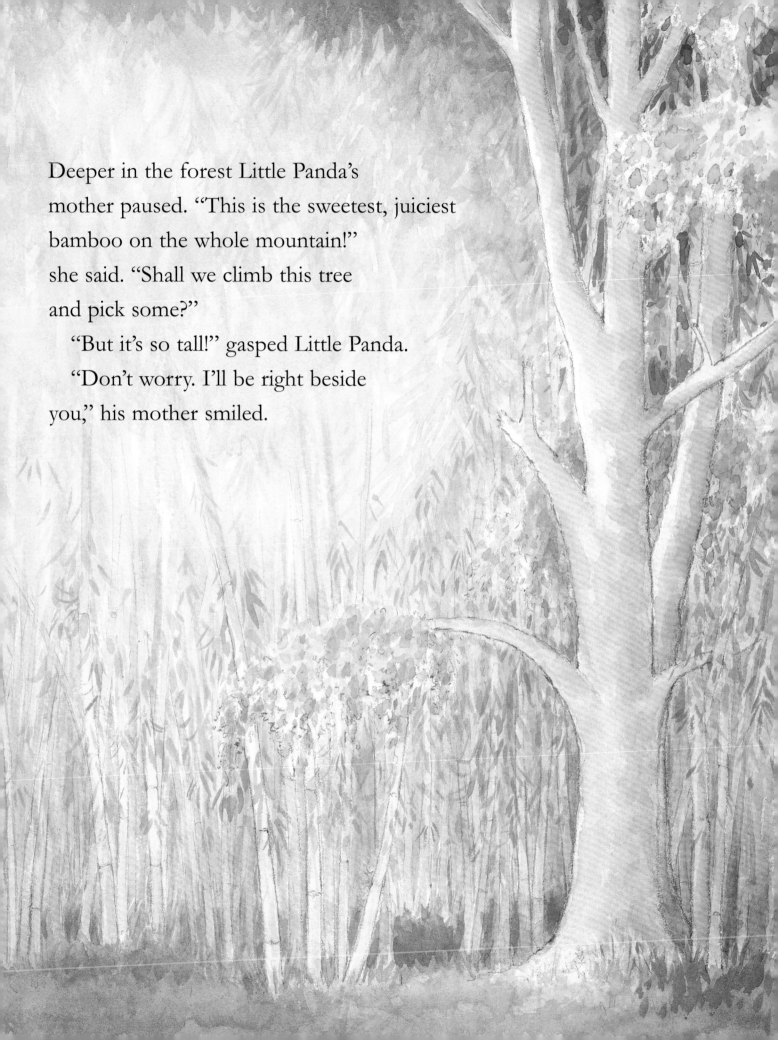

Deeper in the forest Little Panda's
mother paused. "This is the sweetest, juiciest
bamboo on the whole mountain!"
she said. "Shall we climb this tree
and pick some?"

"But it's so tall!" gasped Little Panda.

"Don't worry. I'll be right beside
you," his mother smiled.

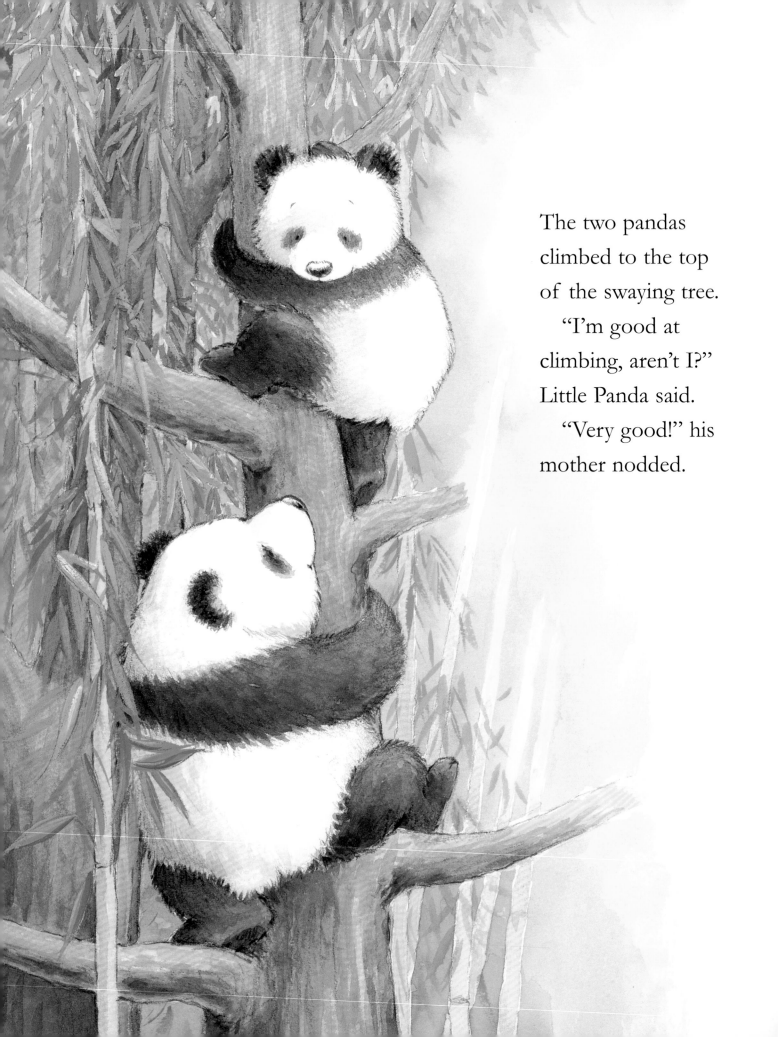

The two pandas
climbed to the top
of the swaying tree.
   "I'm good at
climbing, aren't I?"
Little Panda said.
   "Very good!" his
mother nodded.

They sat in the branches and munched and crunched on
the best bamboo Little Panda had ever tasted!

"I've seen so many new things today," Little Panda said.
"The forest is very big and exciting!"

"I know," Mother Panda laughed. "You're going
to have a lot of fun exploring it all!"

The next day, the two bears walked down
to the Great Pine Forest once more.

Little Panda heard a rustling sound in the trees.
A young panda peek-a-booed him through the
leaves. Little Panda laughed!

"Would you like to go and play with him?" asked
Mother Panda.

Little Panda hesitated . . .

"I'll be here if you need me!" she said.

The friendly panda peeped his
head out through the leaves again!
Little Panda clambered up through the
branches to join him.

Little Panda and his new friend chased
each other through the tall trees and played hide
and seek in the thick bamboo.

They raced down to the stream
and splashed in the cool water.

They rolled dry and lolled in the grass together. It was all great fun!

Then, suddenly, Little Panda heard his mother calling him.

"Time to go home!"

"What, already?" Little Panda cried, scrambling back through the trees.

"We'll come again tomorrow!" Mother Panda laughed.

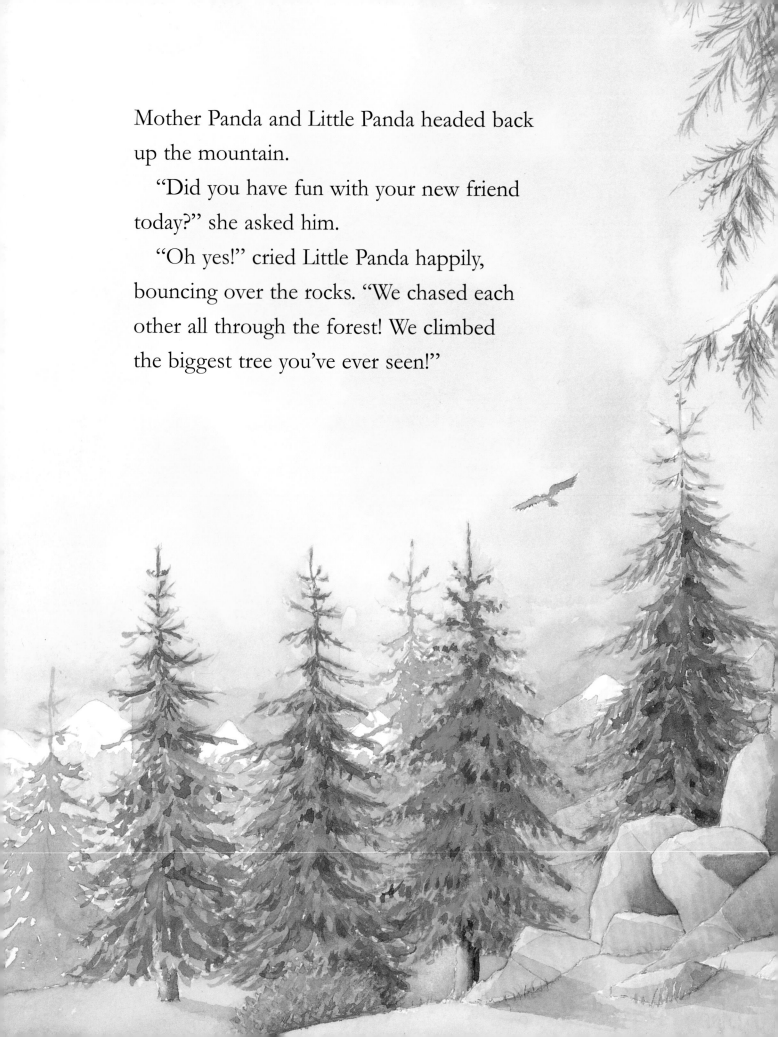

Mother Panda and Little Panda headed back
up the mountain.

"Did you have fun with your new friend
today?" she asked him.

"Oh yes!" cried Little Panda happily,
bouncing over the rocks. "We chased each
other all through the forest! We climbed
the biggest tree you've ever seen!"

Little Panda gazed out across the valley, glowing pink under the setting sun.

"Tomorrow I'm going to explore all the way over to the Big River!" he told his mother sleepily.

Mother Panda smiled as she wrapped her arms around
Little Panda. He closed his eyes and snuggled deep into
her warm fur.

Soon stars began to twinkle in the darkening sky. But
Little Panda didn't see them. He was already fast asleep!